For Liam, Victoria, Leia, and Bayden, bathing artistes
Mom and Barbara, the ultimate career counselors
Linda Johns and Marlene Perez, hand-holders extraordinaire
Craig Shannon, my true companion
—TMS

For Liam, king of the tub, commander of tub toys
—Daddy (TW)

To Yvette, who always seems to make my heart beat
And Roman and Sophia, who never seem to manage to keep the bath water inside the tub
—LC

Text copyright © 2002 by Terry Miller Shannon and Timothy Warner
Illustrations copyright © 2002 by Lee Calderon

Tricycle Press
a little division of Ten Speed Press
P.O. Box 7123
Berkeley, California 94707
www.tenspeed.com

Design by Betsy Stromberg
Typeset in Knock Out

Library of Congress Cataloging-in-Publication Data

Shannon, Terry Miller, 1951-
  Tub toys / by Terry Miller Shannon and Timothy Warner ;
illustrations by Lee Calderon.
    p. cm.
Summary: When his father calls out "Bath time," a young boy
starts gathering all of the toys that will make his bathing fun.
  ISBN 1-58246-066-3
  [1. Baths--Fiction. 2. Toys--Fiction. 3. Stories in rhyme.] I.
Warner, Timothy, 1970- II. Calderon, Lee, 1962-, ill. III. Title.
  PZ8.3.S52915 Tu 2002
  [E]--dc21

2001007363

First printing, 2002
Printed in Singapore

1 2 3 4 5 6 — 06 05 04 03 02

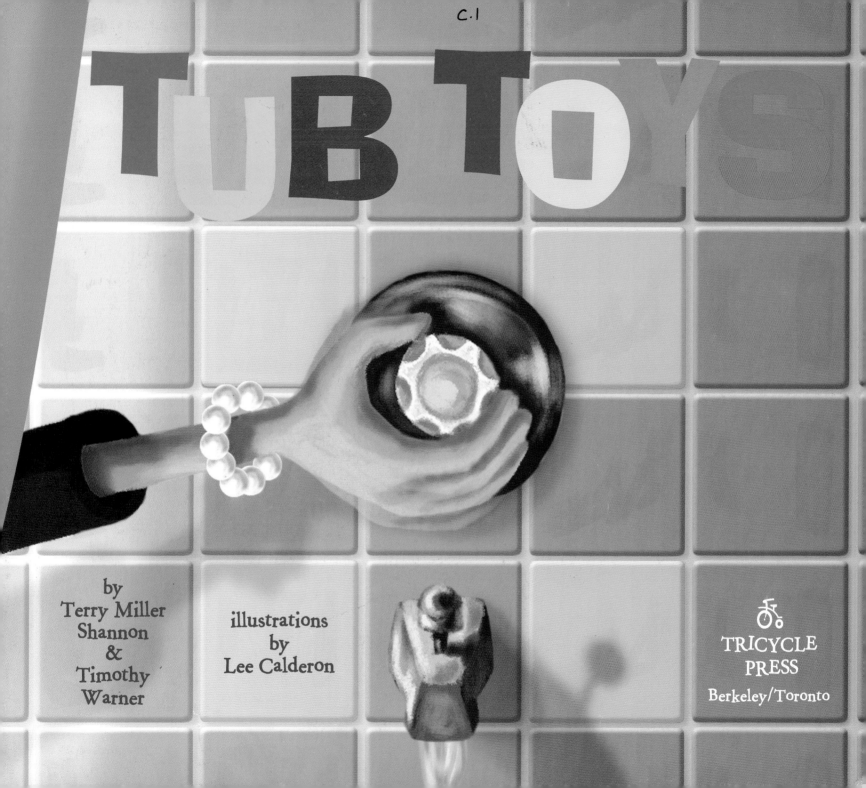

TUB TOYS

by
Terry Miller
Shannon
&
Timothy
Warner

illustrations
by
Lee Calderon

TRICYCLE
PRESS

Berkeley/Toronto

Daddy calls out,
" Bath time! "

The knob squeaks and water pours.

I knock down my block tower
and go racing through the door.

I add his windup froggy friend
so he won't be all alone.

Then I squeeze in extra bubbles, add a beach ball, noodle strainer,

two trucks with
rubber wheels,

and a **huge**
ice cream
container.

My mother says, "Now, **hurry**,
or your water won't be warm."
So I—quick!—toss in an eggbeater to **whip** up a bubble storm.

An empty bottle sure is good,
but **three** would be much better.
Where's that doll who likes to swim? I hurry off to get her.

"Get in!" I hear Daddy call, but I have just begun.
I know I need more tub toys
or my bathing won't be fun.

Splish, splash, splosh, splash!

Four blocks fall through the foam.
And I can't forget my astronaut
inside his spaceship home.

But I can't seem to help myself.
"Need," I gasp, "**five** ships!"

She clears her throat, "Ahem!"
waves her finger in the air,
then points in my direction.

"Your toy box is almost...

bare."

"If you really want me to hurry,
        you can help me," I suggest.

"Bring a spatula and your funnel—

your funnel is the **best!**"

She shakes her head from side to side.

"Looks to me like you have **plenty.**

You've picked so many playthings,

why, there must be more than **twenty!**"

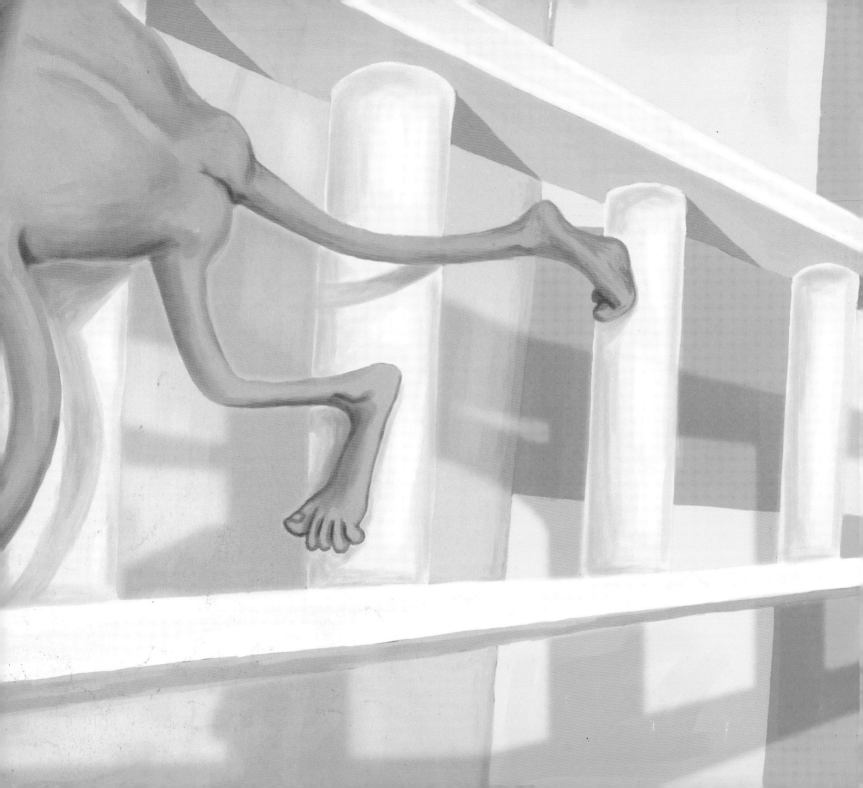

I'm finally climbing in my bath but stop at what I see.

The tub is crammed so full of toys

there's not a spot for me!